THE WHISPER AND THE RUNAWAY

JM TANGARD

STAUNTON PRESS

The Whisper and The Runaway

Episode on in a short series: The Whisper

Published by Staunton Press

Print ISBN: Paperback 978-1-972492-04-8

Ebook ISBN: 978-1-972492-05-5

This is a work of fiction. Names, characters, places, and incidents are either the products of the author's imagination or are used fictitiously. Any resemblance to actual persons, living or dead, businesses, companies, events, or locales is entirely coincidental.

Cover design by Karine Green

CONTENTS

1. THE LIBRARY 1

2. JACKIE RAGE AND THE NIGHT MARKET 11

3. MARLEY ON THE RUN 18

4. THE FIRST INTERVENTION 26

5. THE STALL 34

6. NO SAFE DIRECTION 39

7. THE RAGE REPORT 48

8. FIFTEEN BLOCKS 53

9. ARCHIVES 59

10. THE DETROIT PRESS: Vivi Marsh 69

11. City Tablet Set Up 75

12. MARLEY'S MORNING 89

13. Marley's English Project, Six Months Later 99

Chapter One

The Library

The public library was the only place in the city where Marley Stevenson felt like she could breathe. Not because it was quiet. It wasn't. Not anymore. The modern library was a living organism, full of motion and more noise than of days passed, even if still quiet. Kids argued over computer time. Adults hovered near the copiers with forms they didn't understand. Teen interns like Marley drifted between shelves with carts full of returns. Phones chimed, only to be hastily silenced. The air smelled faintly of coffee, toner, and the citrus cleaner the janitors used on the floors, and of course, old books. Computer tables hummed in the background.

Marley liked the low noise of the bustle. Noise meant she could disappear. It was also clean and elegant here. It made her feel like she wanted to learn and would enjoy it if life allowed it.

She had been practicing the skill of not being noticed since she was seven, moving through four foster homes with the same quiet efficiency she brought to the circulation desk. Both of her parents had been killed by a drunk driver. Neither had relatives, and while her mother's friend had been a good babysitter, she couldn't take care of Marley full-time. With no one else, the foster care system gained a new kid.

The current placement, a split-level off Dennison Avenue, ran on three simple rules: don't make noise, pretend not to exist, and never ask for anything. Marley followed them exactly. In exchange, Sandra and Roy collected their monthly check, gave her just enough money to keep social workers off their backs, and left her alone. It wasn't a home or a refuge. It was a roof that kept rain off her head, sometimes, but basically, she was left to fend for herself. The library was everything else.

Her library workstation sat behind the circulation desk, a narrow strip of laminate just wide enough for the laptop, barcode scanner, and a pegboard of headphones. The desk lamp cast a warm circle of light across her sketchbook, half hidden under the monitor. She kept it there like a secret. Whenever no one was looking, she slid it out and added quick lines to a drawing she had started earlier: a mother with tired eyes and a little boy tugging at her sleeve. Graphite made the world slower. It gave her something solid to hold onto.

Sometimes she would even sketch people from the newspapers the library still kept.

"Marley, can you help me with this?" a man called from the printer station.

She slipped the sketchbook away and stood. "Sure. What's going on?"

"It says the job is stuck in the queue. I need a personal copy of my quarterly taxes." He incessantly pressed the copy button as if that would unjam it.

"No worries. I'm sure we can get it working."

She cleared the queue with a few clicks. He thanked her and hurried off. Marley returned to her cart and fell into the rhythm: scan, stamp, sort.

The front doors opened with a soft hiss. A city official stepped inside. Marley recognized him from the posters near the community board. He looked smaller in person, nervous. He moved quickly toward the reference stacks, glancing over his shoulder.

A man in a tailored suit entered moments later. He walked with a calm that felt unnatural in the busy room. His hair was neatly styled, his expression unreadable. Marley had seen his face before. Not in person. On the news. Mark Freeling. A fixer. A man who made problems vanish for people who could afford him. He'd been on a Documentary called "Detroit: Paris of the Midwest."

She returned to the desk.

"Marley, can you help with these?" The librarian pushed a cart of returns toward her.

"I would love to." She smiled as she pushed the cart toward the aisle, noticing the politician in the next row over.

She tried to focus on her work, but her eyes kept drifting toward the corner where the two men stood. Their whispered voices carried just enough to reach her.

"You said you handled it," the official whispered.

"I did," Freeling replied. His tone was soft, almost gentle. "But you created a new problem."

"I didn't mean to. I just, what happened to Buckley? I don't want that to happen again. I need to know it's contained."

A silence that had weight to it.

"It's contained," Freeling said. "Don't say that name again. It's an old problem. Let's focus on your new one."

Marley's hands went still on the scanner. She did not look up. She leaned her head down enough to allow her long braids to block her face as she cornered her eyes to look at them indiscreetly.

Freeling passed the official a small envelope. The official's face went pale.

"You'll take care of it," Freeling said. "Or I will."

The barcode scanner beeped sharply in Marley's hand. She hadn't pressed anything. The sound came out of nowhere, bright and loud in the quiet aisle.

Freeling's gaze lifted. Unhurried. As if already certain of what he would find.

Then Freeling moved.

Not fast. That was the part that made her stomach drop. He moved the way water moved, finding the path of least resistance, unhurried, inevitable. He handed the envelope to Birch without looking at him and stepped into the aisle.

Marley set the scanner down on the cart.

She heard Birch say something behind him. Something about Marsh. Freeling's answer was three words, dismissive, the tone of a man closing a file.

"Already taken care of."

Marley turned and walked toward the reference section. Not running. Walking. She had learned the difference early. Running said guilty. Walking said somewhere to be.

She returned to the front desk. There were adults there. It was her experience that adults who meant harm backed off when random, unknown adults were around.

She heard his footsteps behind her, and true to her experience he kept walking out the door.

When her shift ended, she went to her workstation. She closed her sketchbook, the one with the mother and the little boy and the half-finished drawing she would never finish now, and slid it into her backpack. She added her charger. Her phone. The three protein bars she kept for nights when Sandra and Roy forgot to leave anything out.

She zipped the bag and put it on, just in case it rained.

She walked toward the front entrance.

Freeling was waiting near the display case by the door. He had his coat on. He looked like a man waiting for a friend, patient and unhurried, the way he looked at everything.

"I'll drive you home," he said. Quiet. Polite. Not a question.

Marley looked at him.

"My ride's already outside," she said, retreating back inside to the main desk. The librarian had already left. She was alone.

"Oh, I don't think so, little foster girl. Marley, is that your name? Or do you prefer your full name, Marlanique?"

She turned left at the end of the aisle, into the periodicals room. The door to the archive hallway was on the far side, past the newspaper racks and the reading tables. She knew this room the way she knew every room in the library. She had been disappearing into it for two years.

She went right instead of straight, behind the microfiche cabinets, and crouched below the level of the reading table. She pressed herself against the cabinet's metal side and held completely still.

Freeling's footsteps crossed the threshold. Stopped.

She heard him breathing. Measured. Patient. The footsteps moved left, toward the window alcove.

She moved right. Low and quiet, behind the second cabinet, then the newspaper rack, then through the archive hallway door, pulling it shut behind her without letting the latch click.

She walked the length of the hallway, pushed through the side exit, and stepped into the cool street air.

She didn't stop moving until the library was three blocks behind her.

She was shaking. Not from fear, or not only from fear. From something else underneath it. Her legs were steady. Her breathing was coming back. She had been in a room with Mark Freeling, and she had walked out of it on her own two feet.

She knew two things she hadn't known twenty minutes ago.

Someone named Buckley was a problem that had already been handled.

Someone named Marsh was a problem that Freeling believed was already handled, too.

She didn't know what either of those things meant yet. But she was a library intern. She knew how to find out.

The Poletown East neighborhood swallowed her with the roar of traffic overhead. Concrete pillars rose like gray trees, covered in graffiti and old posters. The air smelled of oil and damp earth. Marley found an abandoned maintenance room, slipped inside, and shut the door. Her breath was evening out now. She slid down the wall and pulled out her sketchbook.

Her hands were steadier than she expected.

She quickly drew her sketches: first Freeling's face, the jawline, the eyes, the calm that never wavered even as he followed her. Then she moved to Birch, the pale face, the envelope changing hands. She carefully traced her path through the periodicals, identifying the cabinet, the door, and the exact moment she made her move. She made cartoon bubbles and drew in their conversation.

She drew it all before she could forget it.

She needed help. Not the police. Not anyone who could be bought. But she also needed a library database and fifteen minutes, because she had two names and she knew how to use a search index.

Her phone buzzed.

She almost dropped it. She hadn't texted anyone. She hadn't called anyone. The screen showed a single notification from an app she didn't recognize, no icon, no name, just a gray rectangle where the logo should have been.

One line of text.

You are not the only one watching him.

Marley stared at it. Her thumb hovered over the screen. When she tapped the notification, it opened to nothing. A blank interface. A cursor blinking in an empty text field.

She looked around the maintenance room. Concrete walls. A rusted door. No windows. No one.

She looked back at the screen.

Her hands were still shaking when she typed: *Who are you?*

The cursor blinked for a long moment.

Then: *Leave a message where you found safety today. You'll know the right place.*

The app closed. When she looked for it again, it was gone. No trace in her recent apps, no notification history. As if it had never existed.

Marley sat very still.

She didn't know what had just happened. She only knew that something had found her before she had found it. And whatever it was had been watching Freeling long enough to know she wasn't the only one.

She closed her sketchbook and held it to her chest.

The urban legends book. That was where she had found safety today. The library. How long had this person been watching the library?

She pulled the borrowed book out of her backpack and headed back toward the library.

Chapter Two

Jackie Rage and the Night Market

The Night Market lived in the cracks of the city, in alleys behind shuttered storefronts and beneath strings of mismatched bulbs that flickered like uncertain promises. It opened only after dark, when the official city went to sleep, and the real one woke up in a different place every night.

Jackie Rage thrived here.

Her stall was a riot of color and noise. Old phones, cracked tablets, and half-functional laptops sat stacked beside bins of cables and chargers. A small speaker played a playlist she claimed was curated by "the ghosts of the internet." Used designer bags, the real ones, not the knockoffs, sat on a separate table behind her. Anything that could carry information in it and be casually exchanged.

She wore a jacket covered in patches and pins, each one a story she would tell for the right price. Some were on Velcro, so she could change them, signaling an update in information.

Jackie didn't sell hardware. The hardware was just camouflage.

Jackie was sorting through a pile of gossip that her team had found in the whispers when she noticed the library volunteer hovering near her stall. She recognized him. He came through most Thursdays hunting cheap charging cables and occasionally selling details about lost-and-found items that never reached the official desk. Tonight, he stood too still, clutching a book as if it might bite him.

"You lost?" Jackie asked, not looking up from the cracked phone, she was prying open to get the small envelope out. If luck held out, she'd know who the mayor's lover was and be able to leverage it for more housing funding.

He held a book in both hands like it might bite him. "Someone left this in the drop bin. I thought you'd want to see it."

Jackie raised an eyebrow. "You brought me a library book."

"Just look inside." He held it out to her.

She sighed, wiped her hands on her jeans, and took it. It was a paperback on urban legends, cover creased, spine cracked. When she flipped it open, a folded piece of paper slid out.

Jackie caught it before it hit the ground.

The volunteer shifted nervously. "I didn't read it. I just... something felt wrong."

Jackie unfolded the paper. A sketch stared back at her in quick, desperate strokes: sharp jaw, cold eyes, an expensive suit that looked out of place even on paper.

She knew that face.

Mark Freeling.

Her stomach tightened. She flipped the paper over. A message was scrawled on the back in shaky handwriting.

Please. I saw something. He saw me. I can't go to the police. My foster parents won't help. I don't know where else to go. He knows who I am.

Jackie exhaled slowly. "Where did you find this?"

"In the drop bin. It was inside that book."

"Who brought it in?"

"I don't know. It wasn't checked out. It was just... there. There's a girl who works there with me. It looks like her work. I am sorry, I didn't pay attention to her name. We don't often work the same area."

Jackie closed the book and handed it back. "You didn't see anything. You didn't bring me anything. Do you understand?"

He nodded. "Bro, I ain't no snitch"

"Go home." Unsure of that. Seemed he was capable of sharing information if he thought it was important. "Tell one, little whisper, do you understand. And you are working toward something better at the library. Say, 'Ma'am, I do not tell.'"

The volunteer nodded quickly and disappeared into the crowd.

Jackie waited until he was gone, then slipped the sketch into her jacket. She tapped her fingers on the stall counter, thinking. Freeling wasn't the kind of man you stumbled into by accident. If a kid had seen something and Freeling had seen her see it, the kid was already in danger.

She'd grown up in the foster system herself, with a very slappy foster mother and a punchy foster father. This poor kid wouldn't get much help from them. *Oh, to be invisible on that level,* she thought savagely. Sometimes invisibility saved your life; sometimes it cost it.

Jackie didn't like kids. They were unpredictable. Emotional. But she liked loose ends even less. Loose ends got people killed. And Jackie had a reputation to maintain. It was even sadder that all this kid had was Jackie, but it was better than nothing.

She closed her stall early.

The Night Market's atmosphere shifted around her as she walked. Vendors called out prices. People argued over counterfeit IDs. A man with a suitcase full of watches tried to sell her one. She ignored them all and headed toward a narrow alley behind a row of shuttered shops.

She headed toward a narrow alley behind a row of shuttered shops. The alley was empty except for a single metal door with peeling paint. Jackie knocked twice, paused, then knocked once more.

The door opened a crack. A pair of eyes peered out.

"You again," the voice said.

"Miss me?" Jackie held up the sketch. "I've got something."

The door opened wider. A hand reached out. Jackie pulled the sketch back.

"Not for you," she said. "For them."

The eyes narrowed. "You sure?"

"Yeah. This one's Whisper business."

The door closed. Jackie waited in the quiet alley, the distant hum of traffic and the buzz of a faulty streetlight the only sounds. She tapped her foot, impatient.

After a minute, the door opened again. A small metal box slid out. Jackie placed the book and the sketch inside and closed the lid. The box disappeared back into the darkness.

Jackie stepped back into the Night Market. The air felt colder now. The lights seemed dimmer. She zipped her jacket up to her chin and walked quickly, her boots crunching on broken glass.

Somewhere in the city, The Whisper would receive the sketch. He would see the fear in the lines, the urgency in the strokes. He would know a kid was running for her life.

Jackie didn't know if The Whisper cared about kids. She didn't know if he cared about anything. But she knew he hated men like Freeling. Had obsessed over them since she'd met him, nearly forty years ago.

And that was enough.

She returned to her stall, reopened it, and pretended nothing had happened. But she kept glancing toward the alley, waiting for a sign. A message. A whisper.

Nothing came.

Not yet.

But Jackie knew better than to expect theatrics. The Whisper didn't announce himself. He didn't show up in person. He didn't need to.

When he moved, the city moved with him.

And somewhere out there, a frightened kid didn't know that she should be hoping The Whisper would move soon.

Chapter Three

Marley on the Run

The abandoned house on Ferry Street had been her refuge since being placed with the new fosters. The front and back were boarded up tight, but the basement behind the overgrown bush had an open window. She slid in, making her way up the stairs.

It was a shame this house lay in shambles. It had good bones and was solid. She'd sometimes imagine she was the owner, even cleaning up the living room before painting a bird on it. She'd close her eyes and imagine her parents were still alive, and this was their home. Mom was in the kitchen cooking dinner, and Dad was in the den upstairs working on an important project for work. As long as she kept her eyes closed, she could let herself believe it, if only to truly escape for a few minutes.

She opened her backpack as she sat cross-legged on the floor. She had used the last of her coins to grab a bag of chips out of the vending machine near the library as she left. She ate them one at a time, making them last.

She still had the sketchbook. She still had the message from her phone burned into her memory.

You are not the only one watching him.

The app had known about Freeling before she even left the sketch in the library book. Whatever or whoever sent that message had already been watching him. She had walked into something that was already in motion.

Marley did not sleep that night.

She tried. She curled up in the corner beneath the hearth, backpack as a pillow, sketchbook clutched to her chest. But every time she closed her eyes, Freeling's face appeared. Calm and certain.

She had seen something she wasn't supposed to see. Worse, he had seen her see it.

"Now, I'll have to take care of your security breach as well," he had said.

She couldn't stop thinking about it; as she saw his eyes, she felt they connected with her. Was he going to kill her? Make her disappear? There was no one to notice if she truly went missing. She was just a shifting foster who didn't get the lucky placements.

The city felt different now. Bigger. Louder, and even with Detroit's dangerous reputation, somehow it seemed even more dangerous. Every sound made her flinch. Every shadow felt alive. She kept replaying the moment in the library: the way Freeling's gaze had locked onto hers with no anger, no surprise. He'd seemed more disgusted with the politician than with her, but it would be she who bore the consequences of the politician's indiscretions.

She pressed her forehead against her knees and tried to breathe.

She pulled her knees to her chest and listened to the roar of traffic as it crossed the overpass a few blocks away. The constant traffic seemed to drown out most things. The old house had its own creaks and groans. She had started cataloguing which ones belonged here and which ones didn't.

Was that a raccoon or a human? She looked out the dirty window at a squirrel climbing a tree.

When she woke with a start, faint morning light filtered through the window, but it was still very dark. Her neck and back ached. She sat up slowly and looked around.

The crumpled chip bag she had left beside her the night before was gone.

Not blown away. There was no wind in here. It had simply vanished from where she remembered leaving it. Nothing else had been touched. Her sketchbook was still in her hands. Her small bag remained right beside her.

Someone had been close enough to take it while she slept.

Marley pressed her back harder against the wall. Her pulse beat loud in her ears. She wasn't only afraid. Something else was there too, underneath it. Primal fear, panic, she almost couldn't breathe.

She hadn't noticed. It terrified her that people could just walk up to her in here. Why had she allowed herself to fall asleep?

She opened her sketchbook to a new page. Her hands were steadier than they had been last night. She drew the scene around her: the hearth, the living room, the graffiti bird with outstretched wings she'd painted on the opposite wall last month. She drew the exact spot where the wrapper had been.

Then she drew the shadow she had noticed the night before. The one that hadn't moved with the changing light. The one she had tried to convince herself wasn't there.

She stared at the finished drawing.

She hadn't imagined it.

Marley closed the sketchbook and held it to her chest.

"I left the message," she said quietly. "I did what you said."

The house gave no answer.

Then, somewhere above her, a pipe shifted. A single soft sound in the metal above her. The kind of sound that could have been nothing.

Marley exhaled slowly. Raccoon! A raccoon had taken her chip bag. The tiny footprints of a quadruped ran across the roof, probably having come in and out of the hole in the roof.

By the time it was fully light, her stomach ached with hunger. She forced herself out of the basement and moved through the maze of vacant lots, staying in the shadows.

She kept moving.

By midday, she realized she was being followed.

It started as a prickle at the back of her neck. She glanced over her shoulder and saw a man leaning against a utility pole, near the fully abandoned Packard Plant, pretending to check his phone. He was too clean for this part of the city. Too still. Too focused.

Her pulse quickened.

She turned down a narrow walkway between two concrete supports by the railroad tracks and headed toward I-94. When she looked back, he was gone.

Another man had taken his place. Older, shaved head, jacket that didn't fit. His eyes flicked toward her every few seconds.

Marley ducked behind a support for the Saginaw overpass, pressing herself against the cold concrete. Her hands shook. She clutched her sketchbook like a shield.

A voice drifted through the air.

Not a whisper. Just a faint distortion in the soundscape, like an echo carried on wind that wasn't there. Marley froze.

The man with the shaved head stopped. He tilted his head, listening.

"You lost, or something?" he seemed to be looking next to her and not at her.

Another sound came. A soft, deliberate footstep. Then another. The acoustics of the Underpass twisted the noise, bouncing it off pillars and walls so it seemed to come from everywhere at once.

The man stiffened. "Who's there with you?"

Silence.

She looked next to her but didn't see anyone. Just what she needed, a lunatic, detached from reality. She should have walked south, not north, toward Packard.

Then a voice answered him. Soft. Calm. Close. She couldn't make out what it was saying, or if it was male or female.

Too close.

The man spun around, eyes wide with terror. He muttered something under his breath. The voice answered again from a different direction, then another. The words were too low for Marley to catch, but their effect was clear.

The man bolted, running toward the street. His footsteps echoed and faded.

Marley stayed hidden, hand pressed over her mouth as her nostrils flared to take in air, until the sound disappeared completely. Only then did she step out from behind the pillar. Her legs trembled.

She whispered, "Thank you."

The Underpass did not answer.

But she felt it. Something in the stillness that didn't feel like being hunted.

She looked around. The space was empty. Silent. Still.

Yet she knew she wasn't alone. Who had that man been looking at? She looked both ways before stepping out from behind the pillar.

She didn't push it away.

She took a deep breath and kept walking. The sound of her own footsteps was the only thing she heard. But she didn't look back.

Chapter Four

The First Intervention

Marley didn't know how long she had been walking. The roar of I-94 and I-75 as the two highways merged overhead never changed. The light filtered through the concrete in thin, fractured beams that told her nothing about the time. Her legs ached. Her throat burned with thirst. She kept moving anyway.

She turned back toward Poletown East, away from Hamtramck, away from the men she'd spotted twice in the last hour. She was starting to understand their pattern. They moved outward from a center point. Which meant if she could figure out where the center was, she could move perpendicular to it instead of directly away. She pulled out her sketchbook and drew it. A rough grid. Intersections where she'd seen them. Vectors.

It wasn't much. But it was hers.

She paused at the edge of a support pillar and checked her phone. Three percent battery remaining. She had a portable charger in her bag, but she needed to stay still long enough to use it, and she hadn't been still long enough for anything.

She thought about Sandra and Roy.

She didn't want to. They weren't the kind of people she chose to think about. Sandra took the check, and Roy watched television, neither of them having looked directly at her for six weeks. But Freeling had been in that library. He had looked at her the way he looked at problems. And in his world, problems had addresses.

And the librarian was proud of her program and would most likely use her name. But he already had her full given name. All he needed was a last name and an address. She doubted the librarian would cough that up, but that city official could probably easily walk in and get the intern records.

They don't define me, she thought. *I define me*.

But that didn't mean she could let them get hurt for something she'd stumbled into.

She plugged in the charger, crouched behind the pillar, and typed a text to Sandra's number.

"Don't answer the door for anyone you don't know. Don't talk to anyone asking about me. I'm fine. Just stay inside tonight."

She stared at it for a moment. Then sent it.

The reply came back in forty seconds.

"Of course, sweetheart. We were so worried. Are you safe? Where are you? We can pick you up."

Marley read it twice. No bull emojis followed by a poop emoji with a winking eye.

Sandra had never called her sweetheart. Not once. Not in six weeks. Sandra called her "the girl" when talking to Roy and "Marley" only when she had to, and nothing at all the rest of the time. They didn't own a working car, and that alone would stop them from offering to pick her up.

She powered the phone off without answering.

Her hands were very still on the phone's dark screen. She thought about what that meant. Someone had Sandra's phone. Someone who knew she was a teenager. Someone who had guessed, correctly, that a foster kid might respond to warmth she'd never actually received.

She powered down the phone and put it in her bag. She would not turn it on again until she had to.

She picked up the sketchbook and kept moving.

She found the passage by accident or through the logic of the space. She had been mentally mapping Freeling's men's positions and moving perpendicular to their pattern, which led her deeper into the underpass maze rather than toward the street. The pillars grew thicker here. The light shifted. The air felt different, cooler. Still, in a way, the rest of the underpass wasn't as the tires gnawed at the seals in the cement.

She almost missed the alcove entirely. It was sheltered behind two leaning pillars at an angle that made it invisible from any of the main paths. She wouldn't have found it if she hadn't been moving diagonally.

She stopped in the entrance and looked.

A blanket. Folded, not discarded. A sealed water bottle, the kind from a store, not a fountain. A single sheet of paper tucked flat beneath the bottle's weight.

Someone had been here recently. Not to hide. To prepare.

She stood in the entrance for a long moment without going in. She checked the angles. She looked at the ground. She looked at the ceiling. Then she stepped inside and crouched beside the bottle.

She picked it up. Cold, clean, new. She drank half of it in one long pull and made herself stop.

Then she picked up the paper.

A photograph, printed in black and white, grainy the way security camera images always are. The library. Shot from across the street, through traffic, from far enough back that whoever took it didn't want to be seen doing it.

Freeling was in the frame. Walking toward the entrance. Unhurried. Certain.

In the bottom right corner, in small precise handwriting, was a date.

Marley counted back.

Six weeks before she had ever seen his face.

Six weeks. Whoever had left this here had been watching Freeling since before she knew his name. Since before the scanner beeped in her hand. Since before any of this.

She hadn't triggered anything. She had walked into the middle of something already running.

She opened her sketchbook to a fresh page and drew the photograph. Not copied it. Drew what she saw in it. The angle. The distance. The patience in the framing. Then she wrote the date beside it and underneath, in small letters: six weeks before me.

She wrote the two names she had been carrying since the library.

Buckley. Marsh.

She stared at them. She had wanted to search them tonight, but the phone was off, the charger was slow, and she didn't trust the signal in here anyway.

She would find a library. Not her library, not for a while, but Detroit had branches. She knew which ones stayed open late. She knew which librarians didn't ask questions. That was tomorrow's problem. Tonight the problem was staying unseen long enough to have a tomorrow.

Then it came.

Not from her phone. Not from any direction she could name precisely.

"You're not alone," the voice said.

Marley did not move. She did not look for the source. She almost answered. Then she understood. One way. She was receiving, not transmitting. She smirked at herself for almost talking back to an old Civil Defense speaker on the wall.

"The text was the right call," the voice said. "It wasn't Sandra."

She went still. He had seen her send it. Not through some distant pole camera. Through her own phone, the same device the app had used. He had been reading her screen the whole time. And if she was right about him, there was only one house on her street that had a Ring camera on Dennison Avenue. It was across the street. He had already seen who was inside that house before she ever typed the first word.

He wasn't responding to her. He was telling her what he already knew, and what she had just confirmed for both of them.

She looked at the photograph. At the date in the corner. At six weeks of watching, that had been running parallel to her life without her knowing it.

"I am sorry I have to be so careful. Right now, you should sleep," the voice said. "You mapped their pattern correctly. They won't reach this section tonight. The blanket is dry. Once I am sure I can trust you, I'll be able to provide more for you."

The resonance faded. The alcove went quiet. The underpass returned to its usual sounds. Traffic overhead. A distant siren. The creak of the city's bones as they settle.

Marley folded the photograph carefully and pressed it inside her sketchbook next to the drawing of Freeling's face and the grid map she had worked out herself. The portrait. The surveillance. The pattern.

Three ways of seeing the same dangerous situation.

She wrapped the blanket around her shoulders and sat against the pillar with the sketchbook in her lap.

She thought about Sandra's phone in someone else's hand. About the word sweetheart typed by fingers that had never been kind to anyone. About what it meant that they were already there, already inside the address they had for her.

Then she opened the sketchbook one more time and wrote underneath Buckley and Marsh a third line.

They don't define me.

She closed the book.

She slept.

Chapter Five

The Stall

Mark Freeling arrived at Jackie's stall a little after ten.

She saw him coming from half a block out. That was the point of the stall's placement. Sightlines in every direction, enough foot traffic to make a quiet conversation look ordinary, enough noise to keep it from carrying too far. She had chosen this corner the first week she ever ran a market stall, when she was seventeen and selling refurbished prepaid phones to people who needed to call someone without anyone knowing they'd called.

She hadn't stopped needing that sightline since.

She kept her hands busy with a cracked tablet she was pretending to strip for parts. When he reached the stall, she glanced up with the same mild expression she gave every customer who wasn't a problem yet.

"Freeling," she said. For a white man, he looked paler than normal.

"Jackie." He set his hands on the edge of the table, unhurried. He was wearing the good coat tonight. That meant he was working and armed more than usual. "I need a phone."

"You always need a phone." She smiled, pleasantly, but already knew that nothing good could come to her from this conversation.

"I need one from the last two weeks. Anything that came in from the area around the main library will do."

Jackie set down the tablet and pulled a plastic bin from under the counter. She sorted through it slowly, taking her time. Three phones, two cracked, one missing its back casing. She lined them up without comment.

Freeling looked at them, not touching.

"The library," Jackie said. "Something happen over there?"

"Routine," he said.

She had learned a long time ago that when Freeling said routine, he meant the opposite. She also knew better than to say so. She pushed the phone without a casing toward him. "That one came in Thursday. Don't know who from. The usual drop in the back of the trash can out front."

He picked it up. Turned it over. The battery contacts were corroded but intact. He slipped it into his jacket and set the usual fee on the table. She pocketed it.

"I'm also looking for someone," he said. "A girl. Teenager. She may have come through the market in the last day or two. Slight. Carries a sketchbook. Light-skinned, African-American, long braids with what appear to be Central High colors woven into them. Dark brown eyes, polite, well-spoken. Runaway, might be in danger."

Jackie kept her face still. *In danger from whom?* This was the part of her work that nobody saw, the part that happened entirely behind the eyes. She was running the calculation already. What he knew. What he thought she knew. What could she give him that would cost Marley nothing?

"Teenagers come through here every night," she said.

"This one is specific." He paused. "She saw something she shouldn't have."

"Ah." Jackie pulled the bin back under the counter. "That kind of specific."

"She left a note somewhere. Someone picked it up and moved it. I want to know where it went."

Jackie wondered about the metal box. The door in the alley. The volunteer's nervous hands holding out the book.

She considered all of that and kept it exactly where it was, behind her eyes, nowhere near her face.

"I hear things," she said. "I don't always hear everything."

"You hear more than most." He smiled, flashing what would be handsome blue eyes if she didn't know him better.

"Flattery." She almost smiled. "What did the note say?"

"That she was frightened. That she'd seen something. That she didn't know where to go." He tilted his head slightly. "The usual things frightened people say."

"And you want to find her before she says them to someone else."

"I want to find her," Freeling said, "before whoever picked up that note does."

Jackie looked at him. His expression was patient, as it always was. That was the thing about Freeling that most people misread. They thought the calm meant he didn't care. Jackie had been watching him long enough to know the calm was the caring. This mattered to him. That made it more dangerous, not less.

"I'll ask around," she said.

"I know you will." He pulled a few folded bills from his pocket and set them on the table without looking at them. "I'd appreciate speed. Meanwhile, for your time and good company." He pushed the bills toward. "A gesture of goodwill."

He left the way he came. Unhurried, as if already thinking about the next thing.

Jackie waited until he was two stalls down before she exhaled. She picked up the bills and pocketed it without unfolding them. Then she looked toward the alley where the metal door was, and away again quickly, in case anyone was watching her watch it.

She thought about the girl's note. *I don't know where else to go.*

She picked up the tablet again and went back to work.

Chapter Six

No Safe Direction

The app appeared at 4:23 in the morning, awaking Marley as the screen lit up. The same gray rectangle, no icon, no name. One line of text.

Move. Do not use the street. Police have a description.

Marley stared at it. Her mouth went dry. *The police!*

She thought about what that meant. A police report meant a story. A story meant someone had given them something to work with. And the only someone who would bother was the man from the library, the one who had looked at her across the room, knowing she'd overheard too much. The fosters wouldn't report her. In fact, once it came to light that they didn't report her, she'd probably be moved on to foster home six.

She tried not to think about what Freeling's men might do if they went to Dennison Avenue looking for her and found Sandra and Roy instead. She pushed the thought away. Sandra and Roy were adults. They could handle themselves. Probably.

Maybe there was a way to get placed in the suburbs? Saint Claire Shores, Auburn Hills, or Southfield. It wasn't like she didn't know how to change schools.

The app closed. She looked for it in her recent apps. Gone.

She was already moving, gathering everything up, unplugging her phone from the portable charger, and stuffing it into her backpack.

The street was wrong from the moment she stepped onto it.

A cruiser rolled slowly two blocks north, headlights cutting through the early gray. It wasn't rushing. It was looking. That was worse. The officer was paying attention and probably knew this area as well as she did, if not better.

She pulled back into the alley beside the shuttered print shop and pressed herself against the bricks. She waited until the cruiser's lights swept past the far end of the block and then moved again, cutting south through the vacant lot between two half-collapsed houses.

Poletown East in the early dawn felt like the bones of something that used to be alive. The lots where houses had stood were flat and grassed over now, the concrete foundations still visible at the edges. Some had been turned into community gardens, raised beds gone dormant for the season, chicken wire and wooden stakes casting long shadows in the early light. Others were just open ground. The kind of space that gave a person nowhere to hide.

She kept to the edges. Foundation remnants. Garden borders. Anything that broke her silhouette.

Her phone buzzed once.

East on Trombly Street. Stay low.

She turned east, keeping close to the overgrown brush of a half-fallen fence.

She saw the first of what had to be Freeling's men at the corner of Trombly and Lyman. He was leaning against a chain-link fence, hood up, pretending to look at his phone. He was doing it wrong. He kept glancing up at the wrong rhythm. She'd been to four different middle schools and two high schools so far. She knew when people were using their phones as a distraction to appear busy while paying attention to something else.

She cut north through a gap between a collapsed garage and a standing one, crossing a yard that had been someone's backyard once. A rusted swing set stood in the middle of it. One swing still hung from the bar, turning slightly in the breeze.

She didn't stop.

The phone buzzed.

Stop. Wait.

She stopped behind the standing garage and held still. Her breath fogged in the cold.

Ten seconds passed. Twenty.

She started as a police radio crackled from the far side of the fence. Two officers on foot, moving parallel to her without knowing it. She could hear them talking. About the shift ending. About the girl they were looking for. Described as a Black juvenile female, approximately sixteen, carrying a dark backpack and a sketchbook, suspected of robbing Deputy Mayor Gerald Birch of his wallet and personal property near the Poletown district.

Marley pressed her back against the garage wall.

Deputy Mayor. That was who the politician must have been. She knew the face but hadn't placed it at the time. Now she knew the magnitude of who she saw.

She had seen the deputy mayor and a fixer exchange an envelope and talk about someone named Buckley like he was a problem that had already been solved. And now she was being framed as a robber for overhearing that someone named Marsh would go the same way as Buckley.

She almost laughed. She pressed her hand over her mouth to stop it. Escape to the suburbs? She'd be lucky to avoid spending time in juvenile until she turned twenty-one.

The officers moved on. Their voices faded.

Move. Two blocks north, then east. Stay off, Chene.

She moved.

The next two hours were a geometry problem she solved with her feet as she moved forward, only to double back to avoid moving obstacles.

Freeling's men were working a grid, but not with the police. She could feel it, the way they appeared at intersections in ones and twos, the way a pattern repeated if she watched long enough. They were covering ground systematically, which meant they had a center point they were working outward from.

The police were different. They were responsive. Someone was feeding them small adjustments to their search area. Which meant someone was watching her move.

She didn't know how. She had kept to the alleys, the vacant lots, the spaces between. She had done everything right.

She stopped behind a dumpster in a narrow alley and looked around. Above her, a security camera mounted to the corner of the building stared out at the alley.

Its red light was off, like everything around here. Half the area was a raging comeback story, the other half was forgotten. Why did she have to be on the forgotten side?

She checked her phone. A new message was already there.

They are using the cameras. I am not, but I can still see them. I turned a few off, but it's only a matter of time before they work around and turn them back on.

She read that twice.

He had turned the camera off. Or he had been watching it and she had simply never appeared in its feed. She didn't know which was more unsettling.

But she understood now why the messages came before she reached the problems rather than after. He wasn't following her. He was ahead of her.

Why couldn't he just send an UBER?

She started moving again.

By the time the morning sky lightened to a pale fall gray, she had only covered six blocks. Nine to go. Her legs ached.

Her throat burned with dryness. She had eaten one of the protein bars from the alcove and rationed the second, breaking off small pieces, making them last.

She turned a corner and stopped.

A cruiser sat idling at the far end of the block, engine running, exhaust rising in the cool air. The officer inside was on the radio.

She backed up three steps and turned down a side passage.

And ran directly into one of Freeling's men.

He grabbed her arm.

She wrenched sideways, hard, dropping her shoulder the way she had taught herself years ago at the third foster placement. She came free and ran.

"I got her!" He shouted. Police, not one of Freeling's men.

The patrol car door opened behind her.

She ran faster than she had ever run in her life and prayed her legs didn't get tangled up underneath her.

She didn't know how long she ducked and dodged. Time collapsed into footsteps and breath and the sound of pursuit getting louder, then quieter, then louder again.

She vaulted a low fence and landed in a vacant lot, her knees hitting hard. She scrambled up without stopping. The lot was wide and flat, a former block of houses cleared down to bare earth, and she was completely exposed. She ran straight across it toward the tree line on the far side, a thin row of scrub trees and overgrown brush along what used to be a fence line.

She hit the brush and pushed through and crouched in the shadows on the other side, pressing herself flat in the dead grass.

Behind her, footsteps hit the pavement at the lot's edge.

Two voices. Not the same two.

"She went through there."

"Call it in."

"Which one? Birch's guys or the department?"

A pause.

"Both, but Birch first."

Marley closed her eyes. Breathed through her nose.

Her phone lit up silently in her pocket. She pulled it just far enough to read it.

Stay. Do not move for eleven minutes. Sending someone, be careful, stay small, stay quiet.

She stayed. She counted.

The voices moved away from the lot, then back, then away again. A flashlight beam swept through the brush sixty feet to her left. She went flat.

The light moved on.

By the time she reached eleven minutes, the area had gone quiet.

Move north. There is a building with a blue door at the end of the block. The door is unlocked. Wait inside.

Her heart pounded as she looked both ways before emerging from the bushes, then took off at a run.

She found it. An abandoned commercial building, single story, the blue paint on the door faded to something closer to gray. She slipped inside and stood in the dark, listening.

Nothing.

She slid down the wall and sat on the cold floor. Her legs shook. She pressed the sketchbook to her chest and waited. She swiped at tears as they defiantly ran down her face.

What a mess! How was she going to get out of this?

Somewhere in the city, she had to believe, someone was moving toward her from a different direction entirely.

Chapter Seven

The Rage Report

Jackie heard about the robbery before the police arrived.

That was the thing about the Night Market. Information moved faster than official channels. By the time two plainclothes officers made their way down the main aisle, Jackie already knew the broad shape of it. A city official. A robbery claim. A Black teenage girl as the suspect. Details that didn't quite hang together if you knew anything about how the city actually worked.

She was sorting through a box of tablets when they reached her stall.

The first officer was broad and tired-looking, like he'd stopped believing most of what he was told. His partner was younger, sharper, trying to look casual and not quite managing it. Still too stiff from the academy. No one had shot the white horse out from his "knight's heart," yet.

"Jackie Rage?" the first one said.

"That's the column," she said, not looking up. "You need a cable, or are you here about something else?"

"We're looking for a juvenile. Black female, approximately sixteen. Goes by Marley. Word is she moves through this market."

Jackie set down the tablet. She looked at them directly, the way she had learned to look at official people. Enough attention to be polite. Not enough to seem worried.

"Lot of kids come through here," she said. "Don't know one name Marley." She was sure Marley was fifteen. These two obviously hadn't bothered to talk to the fosters.

"This one's wanted in connection with a robbery. Personal property taken from Deputy Mayor Gerald Birch near the Poletown district."

Jackie looked at them for a moment.

"Deputy Mayor Birch," she said.

"That's right."

"Gerald Birch." She planted her hand firmly on her hip. "A little girl robbed the Deputy Mayor. No security around to take down this impossibly strong vixen?" She raised an eyebrow, squinting the other to offer her most doubtful look.

The first officer's expression didn't change. The younger ones almost did.

“OK, so maybe he got rolled after a pay-for-play tryst,” The first one shrugged. “We have a robbery report; the circumstances around it aren’t clear.”

"We're just asking questions," the younger one shrugged.

"Of course you are." She pulled a box of cables from under the counter. "I see a lot of kids. I don't catalog them. Leave me a card. I'll call if I see someone matching."

The first officer studied her. She met his eyes pleasantly and waited.

"You know how this city works," he said. His voice had shifted. Not threatening. More like a man who was tired of his own assignment. "We got a complaint. We follow it up. Doesn't mean I'm losing sleep over it."

"I know exactly how this city works," Jackie said. “As I grew up here.”

He set a card on the counter. She didn't pick it up.

The younger officer spoke then, quietly, like it wasn't part of the official script. "The girl isn't safe. Whatever she saw, whatever's going on, she's running from more than us. Someone's going to find her first."

Jackie looked at him for a moment longer than she looked at most people.

"I'll keep that in mind," she said.

They left. Jackie watched them until they turned the corner at the far end of the aisle.

Then she picked up the card and put it in her pocket.

She turned to her assistant, a seventeen-year-old named Daz.

"Watch the stall. Don't sell the blue tablet. Don't let anyone look in the back box."

"How long?" he looked up from his phone, standing to take her place.

"However long it takes." She paused, taking out her car keys. "But hopefully, not long"

She zipped her jacket and walked out into the gray morning toward her Cadillac.

She had three questions. Where Marley was now. What route she was taking. And how much of a head start Freeling's people had on the same information.

She turned toward a narrow passage between two shuttered storefronts and pulled out her phone. She opened a contact listed only as R and typed: *Need a route. Northeast Poletown East. Looking for the girl.*

She waited, hand poised over the start button on the dark grey SUV. Grey, the same color as the road. The same color that traffic cameras struggle to see. Unnoticeable, despite the noticeable brand.

The reply came in under a minute. Not from R. The message appeared in an app she hadn't opened.

She already has one. Stay south of Kercheval until I tell you otherwise.

Jackie stared at the screen for a long moment.

Then she put the phone away and changed her route, turning off the GPS. No one was going to follow her. Except she pulled her second phone out of her jacket pocket, for the one she wanted to.

Chapter Eight

FIFTEEN BLOCKS

The blue-door building smelled of motor oil and damp concrete. Marley sat against the far wall and tried to think.

Deputy Mayor Gerald Birch.

She turned the name over. She had seen him in the library, nervous and small, nothing like the posters near the community board made him look. She had heard his voice break when he said Buckley's name like it was something he was trying not to swallow. And now he was the police she was a robber.

She pulled out her sketchbook and opened it to a clean page. Her hands were steadier than they had been in hours. She drew Birch's face from memory, again, the expression he had when he realized she had heard him. The sweating brow. The eyes darting toward Freeling like a dog watching its owner for permission.

She wrote his name beneath it.

She had a name now. She had Freeling's face. She had a six-week surveillance photograph and a note with two names and a number.

If this ever went anywhere, she had something to give.

Her phone lit up.

Time to move. Alley behind this building, north, then cross Trombly on the far side of the median strip. There is a dog. It will not bother you, but don't let it startle you.

She almost smiled at the last line.

She stood, shouldered her backpack, and tucked the sketchbook under her arm.

The alley was narrow and still wet with morning dew. She moved quickly, footsteps light. Above her the sky had gone from gray to a flat, pale white. The kind of Detroit fall morning that looked like the city had been printed in black and white and someone had forgotten to add the vibrant fall colors back in.

She crossed Trombly at a gap in traffic, walking fast but not running. Running drew eyes. She had learned that from her second foster family, who had turned calling the police into a hobby. Only run if there was no other choice. The rest of the time, move like there was a purpose to the day.

She had a destination now.

The median strip was a narrow band of dead grass and bare trees. A large shepherd mix watched her from behind a chain-link fence as she passed. Its tail moved once.

She moved on.

Freeling's man at Chene and the railroad. Cross before he turns.

She crossed. He was looking the other way.

The city was waking up around her. A few cars. A woman walking a small dog in the opposite direction who looked at Marley and then looked away, the forced practiced unseeing of someone who had spent years not noticing things in this neighborhood. A man in work clothes waiting for a bus also "unnoticed" her.

Marley moved through them and kept going.

Six blocks from where she needed to be, she hit the problem.

A patrol car sat at the intersection ahead, engine idling. Not moving. Waiting. The officer inside was facing her direction.

She stopped and stepped sideways behind a telephone pole, pressing her back against it. The pole was narrow. She knew she was visible if he turned his head more than a few degrees.

She didn't breathe.

Her phone buzzed. She couldn't look at it without moving.

She waited.

The patrol car's radio crackled, audible even from half a block away. The officer picked up the handset. His attention shifted to the radio. His head turned slightly away from her.

She moved. Not running. A fast walk, angled away from the cruiser, across the street and into the lot on the far side, a wide empty space where a commercial building had been demolished down to the foundation slab. She crossed the slab at an angle, heading for the corner where a section of old brick wall still stood.

She reached it and turned.

The patrol car hadn't moved.

She exhaled.

Good. Two more blocks. Stay on the east side of the street. You'll see a municipal building. Brown brick, boarded windows, city seal still on the facade. Go around to the back. There is a door at the base of the north wall. Knock twice.

She read it twice.

Knock twice.

For the first time since the library, she felt something other than fear beneath the fear. Something smaller and more specific.

A dark grey Cadillac Escalade seemed to be circling the area. It'd stopped twice near where Marley hid. She checked the phone; there were no mysterious messages. Must be one of Freeling's men, police didn't drive Escalades.

She put the phone in her pocket and started moving.

The Escalade pulled up on the other side of the bush she jumped behind.

"Get in. I don't have time to explain." An older black woman lowered the window, her short braids tinged with grey, with eyes hidden behind dark sunglasses.

Marley didn't move, frozen.

"Now. I don't have time to play with you, girl. Get in the back. Stay on the floor. You are not alone, but you will be if you don't get in."

Marley didn't think. She moved, opening the door and lying down in the back of the SUV. The engine revved as it took off down the street, passing the patrol cars and other men.

Chapter Nine

Archives

Jackie drove without speaking.

She took turns Marley wouldn't have thought to take, moving through the abandoned grid of the old industrial corridor without hesitation. She knew this part of the city the way someone knows a place they've driven through a thousand times without ever stopping. The Escalade's engine was the only sound.

Marley lay on the floor of the back seat and watched the light patterns on the ceiling change. Sky between buildings. The underside of an overpass. Sky again.

The car slowed and turned. The surface beneath the tires shifted from pavement to something rougher, cracked concrete, then stopped.

"Up," Jackie said.

Marley sat up carefully and looked out the window. They were inside the footprint of a demolished block, surrounded on three sides by the remaining walls of buildings that no longer had interiors. Weeds pushed through the concrete. A rusted loading dock door hung at an angle from one hinge. The city felt very far away and very close at the same time.

Jackie pointed through the windshield at an orangish-brown brick building at the far edge of the lot. It looked exactly like a building the city had forgotten. The city seal above the main entrance, faded and chipped, the name of some department Marley couldn't quite read. Plywood over every window. A chain across the main steps that had been there long enough for rust to make it part of the architecture.

"Those stairs on the north side," Jackie said. "Use the app on your phone. You'll know what to do."

Marley looked at her. Jackie was already facing forward again, both hands back on the wheel.

"Thank you," Marley said.

Jackie didn't answer, simply nodding, sunglasses tilted up to the rearview mirror.

Marley reached back and pushed the door open by leaning on it.

Jackie took a few bills out of her pocket.

"Use this only when you need it. Do not spend it on anything that isn't food when you're starving, and the next meal is unknown, or a ride when you're stuck. You hear. Only when you need it. Not to get your braids fixed or buy trendy clothes. Only when your well-being or life is at stake."

Marley nodded, taking the bills. She didn't want to, but this was a survival resource that couldn't be turned down.

Marley got out. The door closed behind her. The Escalade reversed, turned, and moved back toward the street without hurrying. It was out of sight before Marley reached the building's corner.

She moved around it slowly, staying close to the wall. The north side faced an alley running behind a row of vacant lots. No windows on this face. The building's blind side.

The app appeared on her phone before she found the door.

Base of the north wall. Concrete ramp. Green door.

The door was set into the foundation, below grade, accessible by a short concrete ramp that had been invisible from the street. She would have walked past it three times without finding it. A metal door painted a flat institutional green that had faded to almost nothing against the ugly wild bushes that seemed to be growing out of the concrete, hinges dark with rust, she suspected was more cosmetic than real.

She knocked twice.

Nothing.

She waited.

A minute passed. Then another.

The door opened inward. Not fast. Slowly, deliberately.

The space beyond it was dark, except for the red scan light of a camera.

“Confirmed,” an A.I. voice said, serenely.

A voice came from inside. The same male voice from the Underpass. Calm. Precise. Older than she had imagined it.

"Come in, Marley."

She stepped forward, praying this wasn’t some sort of trap.

Inside, her eyes adjusted slowly.

The space was larger than it should have been. A basement level, low ceiling, concrete floors. Fluorescent tubes cast flat white light over rows of metal shelving that ran floor to ceiling on three walls. The shelves held boxes, hundreds of them, identical banker's boxes labeled in a cramped hand she would have needed to step closer to read.

At the center of the room, a long metal table held equipment she could name and equipment she couldn't. Monitors. A radio setup that looked older than she was. Cables running along the floor in organized bundles secured with metal clips.

And at the far end of the table, facing away from her, a man. White hair, close-cropped, and balding on top. Shoulders that had probably been broader once. His hands rested on the table beside a keyboard. The knuckles were large, arthritic looking, like he'd worked with his hands all his life. He wasn't typing. He wasn't moving. He was simply there, the way furniture is there, as if he had always occupied exactly that amount of space and no more.

He did not turn around.

"Sit down," he said. "You've been on your feet for eleven hours. I apologize for that. I had to make sure you weren't tagged before exposing my home."

"You live here?" Marley looked around the space. A chair sat near the door. She had a feeling it had been placed there recently.

He nodded. "Bought this for a song during the city's bankruptcy filing." He smiled. "I don't know if they still say for a song, suffice to say, I got it cheap."

She sat. "I have heard it. Mostly older folks."

For a long moment, neither of them spoke. The equipment hummed. The fluorescent lights buzzed faintly.

"You're the Whisper," she said.

"That's what people call me."

"What do I call you?"

A pause. Not hesitation. More like consideration.

"Whisper will do. I have been called that for the last fifty years," he said. "Not sure my real name is even useful anymore. They may have declared me dead anyway."

Marley looked at the shelves. At the boxes. At the organized patience of all of it.

"Wow, fifty years. How long have you been doing this?" she asked.

He didn't answer right away. When he did, it was not the answer she expected.

"Long enough to know that you don't run when you have the ability to fight, or when someone with Freeling's resources is chasing you. I'll say, you are impressive, though. You have some stealthy dodging skills. I've watched three witnesses go through what you went through in the last two days. You're the first one who didn't get caught by them. How do you learn that maneuver to get away from Freeling's man? Vice Mayor is getting careless."

Marley thought about that.

"My third foster family was a dope ring. They cared for me, but not the most upstanding people. They got busted. My older foster brother taught me how to fight because I was getting bullied at the new school. Yes, the Vice Mayor was shaken. Don't have to be an adult with secret squirrel spy skills to have understood that."

"I suppose you don't, but don't sell your street sense short. It's kept you alive."

"The note said the others ran."

"They did."

"Are they safe?"

A pause.

"One is," he said. "The other I'm still working on locating. You are the only one without any resources. That's the only reason you are here. We need to find you some place safe."

"What about the foster parents?"

"I think you know, but I can say it out loud if you need to hear it."

She looked at the floor. She had thought about it. Once, briefly, in the blue-door building, before she made herself stop. She had decided they could handle themselves.

They couldn't.

"What happened to them is what happens to anyone who tries to punch above their weight without skill."

"I never thought..."

"...To warn them? Why would you? I offered them the same courtesy they would have offered others. But yes, I thought about them. Wondered if Freeling would go for them. Didn't think he would do that."

"Do we have any idea why he would?"

"They tried to bribe him, but he simply reacted to their bribe in a way that powerful hitmen do when confronted with powerless people." He chuckled. "You thought I was the hero? No, sadly, I am just a whisper on the wind. I would like to think I am not the villain, but I am not so foolish as to think I am the hero. I trade the information, though. The video was delivered to Detroit Homicide just after you were dropped off."

The room hummed around them. Somewhere above, Detroit went about its morning.

Marley opened her sketchbook to the page with Birch's face. She looked at it for a moment. Then she set it on the table. Her foster parents dead. She felt bad that she didn't feel more about that revelation.

"I think you should have this," she said.

He was quiet.

"I already know what's in it," he said. "You share everything on your social media."

"I know," she said. "But you should have the parts I don't share on social media."

A long pause. Then his hand moved along the table and stopped at the edge of the sketchbook.

That was all.

"Then a trade." He pulled a leather-bound book off the shelf. "Never used." He set it on the table in front of her.

She picked up the book, a new sketchbook, fancier than anything she'd ever owned.

"Thank you. It's beautiful."

But it was the first time, in all of it, that she had the sense of something shifting. Not in the room. In the agreement between them.

"You haven't had proper rest. Get some sleep," he said. "There's a cot behind the east shelving unit. The protein bars in the blue bin are better than the ones I left in the Underpass. Oh, your library book is there too. You'll have to return that once this is calm enough to exit. They'll hunt you down like the damn IRS over a non-returned library book."

"I know." Marley almost laughed. "Thank you."

"It is my highest pleasure."

She got up, went around the shelving unit, found the cot, and lay down. For the first time in two days, she felt something close to safe. She clutched the new sketchbook to her chest.

Above her, Detroit kept moving, as it always did.

Below it, in a basement full of decades of careful attention, a man picked up a sketchbook and looked at a portrait of a dangerous man drawn by a frightened girl.

He set it down precisely.

He went back to work.

She rolled over to keep the light out of her eyes and closed them.

Chapter Ten

The Detroit Press: Vivi Marsh

Detroit Press

METRO & REGION Wednesday

Street Level

A column by Vivienne Marsh

The Vice Mayor Says a Teenage Girl Robbed Him. His Own Police Report Tells a Different Story.

Gerald Birch filed a robbery complaint. The responding officers had questions. So do I.

Vivienne Marsh | Detroit Press Columnist | DETROIT

Let me tell you what Detroit's Vice Mayor, Gerald Birch, would like you to believe.

He would like you to believe that sometime in the early morning hours of this past week, in the vicinity of the Poletown East corridor, a Black female juvenile, approximately fifteen to sixteen years of age, carrying a dark backpack and a sketchbook, relieved him of his wallet and personal property.

That is the robbery report he filed. Those are the words in it. A sketchbook. The alleged dangerous perpetrator was armed with a sketchbook.

I have been covering this city for nineteen years. I have sat in on arraignments. I have read police reports until the language stopped reporting and started becoming circular. And I want to tell you something about the report Gerald Birch filed, the one that has Detroit Police currently running down a teenage girl through the blocks of Poletown East.

The report does not explain what Gerald Birch was doing there.

"Maybe he got rolled after a pay-for-play tryst," one responding officer told a merchant in the Night Market, according to a source in my network, with a shrug that suggested the department's enthusiasm for this investigation had its limits.

Read that sentence again.

A Detroit police officer, responding to a robbery complaint filed by the city's sitting Vice Mayor, suggested to a third party that the Vice Mayor may have been engaging in a transaction of a commercial and intimate nature at the time of the alleged robbery.

The alleged robber is fifteen years old.

I will let you do that arithmetic yourself.

The Detroit Police Department has not confirmed the officer's remarks. The Vice Mayor's office has not returned calls for comment. A spokesperson for Mayor Tillman's office said only that the matter was "under review," which in this city means exactly nothing and everyone knows it.

But here is what I can tell you, because this city talks to me in ways it does not talk to everyone.

Gerald Birch was not in Poletown East by accident. Birch was seen, by multiple witnesses whose names I am not printing because I would like them to continue breathing, in conversation with a second man. The second man is not named in the robbery report. The second man is not mentioned in the robbery report. The second man does not appear to exist, as far as the official record is concerned.

So, who is this second person? I don't know, and that's unusual in itself. I have been covering this city for nineteen years. I know the names of the people who move power in Detroit the way a cartographer knows coastlines. This man is not on any map I have. He has no public profile, no business filings, no civic record, no footprint of the kind that accumulates naturally when a person simply exists in a city over time. He is either very new to Detroit or very deliberate about leaving nothing behind. In my experience, the second explanation is always the more interesting and dangerous one.

Call our tip line if you have information about who this second man is.

Something was exchanged between these two men in a public building in this city. A witness saw it. That witness is now the subject of a robbery complaint filed by one of the two men she saw. The complaint was filed within hours of the exchange. The complaint names only her. It does not name the second man. It does not explain the exchange. It does not explain what Gerald Birch was doing in Poletown East at all.

A fifteen-year-old girl with a sketchbook did not rob the Vice Mayor of Detroit. The Vice Mayor of Detroit used a robbery report to put a fifteen-year-old girl in the path of a police department that is, at best, indifferent to her safety and, at worst, being directed by the same hands that are already looking for her.

I want to be precise about what I am saying, because precision matters in this city more than it does in cities where the powerful are occasionally held accountable.

I am saying that Gerald Birch filed a false police report. That he filed it to locate a witness. That if the responding officer's remark about the nature of Birch's activities that night has any basis in fact, and if that witness is the age she is reported to be, then the robbery report is the least interesting document in this story.

The most interesting document would be whatever Gerald Birch was handed in that public building, by a man whose name remains unknown at the moment.

Today.

I want that girl found. Safely. I want her found by someone who is not looking for her on Gerald Birch's behalf. I want her found by someone who understands that a teenager with a sketchbook in Poletown East is not a criminal. She is a witness. And in this city, witnesses need looking after.

If you know where she is, you know how to reach me. My information has always moved through this city the way information moves best.

Quietly. And to the right people.

Vivienne Marsh has covered Detroit metro affairs for the Detroit Press since 2005. She can be reached at Detroit Press.

Tips may be submitted anonymously through the Detroit Press secure tip line.

Chapter Eleven

CITY TABLET SET UP

The column ran at six in the morning and was further carried by all three local news stations.

By eight, Jackie had sold eleven phones, three charging cables, and a cracked tablet to a woman who said she was buying it for her nephew and was clearly buying it for herself. By nine, she had heard her own name mentioned twice in adjacent conversations, neither time by someone talking to her. By nine-thirty, she had received four messages on three different phones, none of which required a response, and one folded note slipped under her stall counter by a hand she didn't see, which she read once and burned with the lighter she kept in her left jacket pocket.

It was sensitive information that she couldn't use. But no sense in leaving it lying around.

She went back to sorting tablets.

The new shipment had come in the night before, fourteen units in a plastic bin, a mix of cracked screens and water damage and one that looked completely fine, which was always the most suspicious kind. She worked through them methodically, powering each one up, checking what had been left behind. Most people wiped their devices before selling them. Most people were not as thorough as they believed.

The ninth tablet in the pile belonged to someone who worked in the city's child welfare division. Jackie knew this because the woman's work email was still logged in, and because the tablet had not been wiped at all, only factory reset, which was not the same thing and never had been. Jackie had pulled the email cache before the reset finished scrubbing and found three weeks of correspondence she had not been looking for.

She was still reading when she found the forwarded document. This had to have been stolen, not left by one of her whisperers. The only question would be, how did it get here? Only her team knew where to drop these. Someone had been compromised.

Who? She would worry about that later.

A placement review. A name she recognized. An address she recognized. A flag in the system marked urgent, filed six days ago, requesting emergency reassessment of a foster placement based on welfare check failure and unreported absence.

Marlanique "Marley" Stevenson. Age fifteen. Last confirmed location: the split-level off Dennison Avenue.

Jackie read it twice. Then she forwarded it to a single contact, no message attached, and deleted the sent record. When she was done, she wiped her prints off and tossed it to the back. She'd throw this one away.

The next item was a phone. She powered it up to a set of texts. It was information a private investigator was looking for on a financial scandal at a dying mall. She sent him the information, accepting the money for it via Venmo.

She powered the phone down and set it in the pile she was keeping. Then she reached back into the bin and found what she was actually looking for.

A manila envelope, standard size, tucked flat against the bin's inner wall. Her name on the front in handwriting she didn't recognize, which meant it was from someone who knew better than to use handwriting she would recognize. She didn't open it. She read the single line printed in small type in the lower left corner.

For the right hands. Not yours.

She tucked it into her inside jacket pocket. There was only one person 'right hands' referred to. She'd have to make a trip in a few minutes to deliver it.

The tenth phone in the bin was the one she had held back.

She had told herself it was instinct. Freeling had asked for anything from the library district and she had given him the Thursday drop, corroded contacts and all, because it was the most recent and the least interesting. The tenth phone had come in two days earlier from a different drop point, a coffee shop two blocks from the library's side entrance, and something about the timing had made her keep it. She didn't always know why she kept things. She just knew when to.

She pried the casing off now and pulled the SIM. The screen was cracked but functional. She powered it on while she worked through the next tablet, letting it run in the background.

The tenth phone had loaded.

She picked it up.

The text thread was between two numbers she didn't recognize. But the content was specific enough that it didn't matter. A time. A location. The library, named directly. And then a string of messages that read like a checklist being confirmed item by item.

It was a hit order. Someone wanted the person in the photo "to follow" permanently shut up.

The last message in the thread was a photograph.

Vivienne Marsh. Taken from a car, through a window, from across the street from the Detroit Press building. The angle suggested the photographer had been parked there for a while. The timestamp was four days ago.

Jackie set the phone down on the counter. They were stalking Vivienne. She was going to be another Jerry Buckley.

She picked it up again and read the thread from the beginning.

The third message used Marsh's name directly. The fifth described her routine. The seventh used a word Jackie had seen in certain kinds of communications before, a word that did not mean what it said, and everyone involved understood that.

Contained.

Jackie sat very still for a moment.

The kid hadn't witnessed a handshake. She hadn't stumbled into a bribe, a payoff, or the ordinary machinery of corruption. She had been standing three feet away when a city official handed a known fixer the authorization to kill Vivienne Marsh in the form of a final payment for the job. And then that official had used a robbery report to put the city's police force to work finding the one witness who could place him in that room.

Jackie thought about Freeling sitting across her stall counter two nights ago. Patient. Unhurried. Asking about a girl with a sketchbook, with her school colors woven into her braids.

The phone she had given him.

The phone in her hand.

He had asked for anything from the library district. She had given him one phone. If he was thorough, and he was always thorough, he would eventually account for every device that had moved through her stall in the relevant window. He would find the gap. He would know she had held something back.

Jackie was not sentimental about self-preservation. She had survived this city for fifty-five years by understanding exactly when a situation had moved from manageable to terminal. This was the line. Right here. The phone in her hand was the line.

She powered it off and slipped it into her inside jacket pocket next to the manila envelope.

Then she picked up her own phone and opened her contacts to V.

Vivienne Marsh answered on the second ring.

"It's Jackie Rage," Jackie said. "I have something you need to see. Not on the phone. In person. Today."

A pause.

"How serious," Marsh said.

"Your life," Jackie said. "Serious."

She hung up before Marsh could answer and went back to sorting tablets. Birch was still out there somewhere, probably rehearsing the threat he was going to deliver. Let him come. She now had something considerably larger than his ludicrous robbery report to think about.

The column Marsh would write from what Jackie was about to hand her wouldn't just destroy Birch.

It would make Freeling impossible to ignore. It would bury both of them under the jail.

And somewhere in a basement beneath a forgotten building, an old man with careful hands was going to want to know that the situation had just changed shape entirely.

She reached for the city tablet. Time to get rid of two things and deliver one more.

She looked up.

Gerald Birch was moving through the Night Market like a man who had never been told he wasn't welcome anywhere. His suit was wrong for the hour, wrong for the location, and wrong for a man whose name had been in a newspaper column three hours ago, using language that should have kept him indoors indefinitely. His face was the color of meat left out too long. His eyes found her stall and didn't move.

“Pedo!” Someone shouted somewhere in the throng of customers.

Jackie set down the tablet.

He reached the stall and put both hands on the counter leaning in on her. "You did this," he said, pointing in the direction of the shouter.

"Good morning," Jackie said, fanning her nose. “You know, coffee doesn’t actually get rid of morning breath. Only brushing, my friend. If you need floss, I want you to know, I don’t sell that here.”

"Shut up. I am not your friend. That column. You fed that to Marsh."

"Honey, what on earth made you think we were ever friends. I read the column," Jackie said. "Vivienne Marsh is a thorough journalist. She has a lot of sources in this city. And I have a business to run. Not a friend's café with...coffee."

"Don't." His voice dropped. "Don't do that. I know it was you. The officer talked to you. You passed it on."

"An officer talked to me about a robbery report," Jackie said. "Several people were in earshot. Your officers have loud voices, Councilman. Their uniforms and marked patrol cars naturally attract attention, sometimes good, sometimes not."

"Vice Mayor to you."

"For now." She picked up the eleventh tablet and turned it over. "Shouldn't you be in your office? Seems like a busy morning for you."

His jaw tightened. "You've made a significant mistake."

"Mm." She powered the tablet on. Dead battery. She set it in the discard pile to check the back casing for information later.

"A robbery report," Birch said, his voice dropping further, taking on the texture of someone delivering a threat they've rehearsed. "A false report is a serious charge. Filing a false report has consequences. So does feeding fabricated information to the press."

"I didn't feed Marsh anything fabricated," Jackie said. "The officer said what he said. Ask anyone here. All these booths were open. The robbery report says what it says. Marsh printed what she verified." She looked at him directly in the eye for the first time since he'd arrived.

“Yes, and.. you had this hairbrained idea...”

She put her hand up. "You want to talk about hairbrained ideas, let's talk about the robbery report. You had a fifteen-year-old girl. A foster kid. No family, no resources, no one to file a counter-complaint on her behalf." She tilted her head. "You could have called child services. Endangered runaway. Police would have been looking for her to help her, not chase her. The whole city's machinery, pointed at finding one kid, and everyone would have thanked you for caring. She may have even thanked you for caring, with silence." She paused, whispering the word silence with her finger over her mouth. Then she pointed at him.

"Instead you..."

Quietly, she cut him off. "Instead, you filed a robbery report. Which means anyone who reads it has to ask what you were doing in Poletown East at that hour, alone, that a teenage girl with a sketchbook was able to rob you. Birch, you don't even know how to fake being a hero, honey child."

Birch's face had gone from the color of something left out to the color of something that had never seen sunlight. "You don't know what you're talking about."

"I know what an envelope looks like," Jackie said quietly. "I know what it looks like when a man takes one. I know what it looks like when the man who hands it over has no name and no record and no footprint in a city he's clearly been operating in for a while." She smiled, just slightly. "Vivienne Marsh is going to find his name. She's very good.

She doesn't need me, you, or a scared kid to be able to figure that out."

Birch leaned forward. "I will have this stall shut down. Every tablet, every phone, every cable. I will have you charged with receiving stolen property, and I will make sure that silver tongue of yours is cut out."

She smiled shily, as if he were flirting with her, eyes locked firmly on the men approaching. "You're just trying to butter me up." She winked at him, pointing. "I'd worry about what they have to say."

"Mr. Birch."

The voice came from behind him. He turned.

Two plainclothes officers stood at the entrance to the aisle. The broad tired one from before and a third Jackie hadn't seen. The tired one was holding a document. His expression suggested he was not enjoying his morning. Her thoughts also drifted to the intact city tablet that she was now sure was as stolen plant. She'd have to get rid of it.

"Gerald Birch," the officer said. "We have a warrant."

Birch straightened. His voice recovered its authority from somewhere. "This is harassment. She has stolen city property. This woman has also been spreading defamatory..."

"Sir." The officer's tone did not change. "The warrant is for you."

“Told you,” Jackie shrugged. “You never know how interesting a conversation is going to be down here in the Night Market.”

The Night Market went very quiet as all eyes fell on Birch. Some looked away, others openly gawked.

Birch looked at Jackie.

Jackie looked back at him with an expression of polite neutrality. “Officer, I think the cat has taken his tongue. Can he know what the warrant is for?”

"Making a false 911 call," the officer said. "And one count of filing a fraudulent criminal complaint, and child abuse. There will likely be additional charges pending the state's attorney review of the column's allegations." He paused. "The column was very specific."

Birch's mouth opened. Nothing came out.

Jackie picked up the twelfth tablet.

As the officers moved Birch toward the market entrance, she heard him say something about his lawyer, about the mayor's office, about people who would answer for this. His voice faded into the general noise of the market, resuming its business around him.

She powered on the tablet. Cracked screen but functional. She set it in the keeping pile.

Then she laughed. Not loudly. Not for long. Just once, low and to herself, the way you laugh when something lands exactly where it was always going to land.

She turned to Daz. "Watch the stall." She grabbed the city tablet. Time to get rid of this and deliver something else.

"Again?"

"Again. This was never here." She tapped the tablet before stuffing it in her tote. "I won't be long."

She walked out of the Night Market toward the grey Escalade, her hand resting on the envelope in her inside pocket. She had a dead drop to make. And after that, she had a column to read again more carefully, because Vivienne Marsh had written the phrase *at the moment* after the words *name remains unknown*, and Jackie appreciated precision in a journalist.

Maybe it was time she had a name.

She got in the car and pulled out into the Detroit morning without looking back.

Freeling was still out there, and he was the dangerous one. He was the one who would stop a little girl with school colors in her braids from becoming the adult she deserved to be. He'd kill that baby. Jackie was many things, a party to a hit on a kid, never.

Maybe Marley was luckier than Jackie thought that she was on her side.

Chapter Twelve

Marley's Morning

She woke to the sound of the equipment.

Not an alarm. Not a voice. Just the low, constant hum of things that never stopped running, the radio equipment, the monitors, the cables carrying current through the floor in their careful organized bundles. The coffee machine beeped as it finished.

She lay still for a moment and listened to it. She had slept in a lot of places. She had never slept anywhere that felt like this.

She sat up slowly. The new sketchbook was still in her arms. She set it beside her on the cot and pressed her palms against her eyes until the spots cleared.

The Archive Room was the same. The shelving. The boxes. The flat white light. And at the far end of the table, he was still there, or there again. White hair, close-cropped. The wide knuckles resting beside the keyboard. She couldn't tell if he had slept. She suspected not.

She stood and came around the shelving unit.

He didn't turn around. He said nothing. But one of the monitors on the left side of the table had been angled slightly outward, toward the room rather than the operator. She noticed it because all the others faced him. That one faced her.

She stepped closer and read it.

It was the Detroit Press website. Vivienne Marsh's column. The headline filled the top third of the screen.

She read it standing up, her arms crossed over her chest against the cool of the basement air. She read it slowly, taking in the words as her hand drifted up to cover her mouth. She read the officer's remark and thought about the Night Market and the woman with the braids who had driven a grey Escalade through a demolished block without hesitating. She read the paragraph about the second man with no footprint and felt something cold and clarifying move through her.

She read the last three lines twice.

My information has always moved through this city the way information moves best. Quietly. And to the right people.

She stood there for a moment after she finished.

"The robbery report," she said. "It's over?"

"Nearly, Birch has been arrested. They are still looking for Freeling. They will not find him. You will have to watch out. I am sorry. I wish I could offer more. All I can tell you is that I'll monitor him and alert you when he surfaces again."

"So the police aren't looking for me anymore?"

He was quiet for a moment. Then shaking his head, said, "The report has been formally withdrawn." He pointed to another screen, "Breaking News"

She exhaled. It came out longer than she expected.

"And Freeling? Just vanished?"

He reached out and opened a second window on the monitor beside the column. A transit record. A name she recognized on a passenger manifest, departing Detroit on an early train. The timestamp read 5:47 a.m. She looked at it and thought about a man who moved through a city like he owned it, buying phones from a Night Market stall, passing envelopes in library stacks, certain of everything.

Boarding a train alone before dawn.

"He'll come back," she said.

"No," he said. "Not to this city. Not for this." A pause. "He has other cities. Other work. Men like Freeling don't stop. They relocate. But, he won't soon forget what happened. He has friends here. I have arranged a better foster family for you. They'll be able to see to your security, but don't take learning about situational awareness lightly."

Marley looked at the transit record for another moment. Then she looked at the shelves. The hundreds of boxes. The cramped handwriting on the labels she still hadn't stepped close enough to read.

"Is that what you do?" she asked. "Move them along?"

He considered that. "Sometimes. When the alternative costs more than the city can afford."

She nodded slowly. She picked up the new sketchbook from where she had set it on the edge of the table and held it against her chest.

"What happens to me now?" she asked.

He was quiet long enough that she thought he might not answer. Then he said, "There is an envelope on the cot. It was not there when you got up. It's got all the information for you. Your driver will be here soon."

She went back around the shelving unit.

The cot was the same. The blue bin was the same. But on the thin pillow, positioned precisely where she would see it when she turned, lay a manila envelope. Standard size. Her name on the front.

Not her full name. Not Marlanique Stevenson, the name Sandra used when she was annoyed or Roy used when he was reading off her paperwork. Just Marley. Written in a hand so precise and deliberate it looked like it belonged to another era entirely. The ink was dark blue. The letters did not lean.

She picked it up carefully, almost afraid to open it.

The envelope was not sealed. The flap had been folded in, tucked against itself. She opened it and drew out two pieces of paper.

The first was reassignment to a family in Grosse Pointe, a wealthy suburb adjacent to Detroit. The driver would be there soon to take her to her new home.

The second was old. The paper had gone the color of weak tea, and it was fragile at the folds, decades, not years. It was a mimeograph copy of a newspaper page. The masthead at the top read Detroit Free Press. The date beneath it read July 24, 1930. She had to angle it toward the fluorescent light to make out the headline.

BUCKLEY SHOT DEAD IN LASALLE LOBBY.

She sat down on the cot.

She pictured Gerald (Jerry) Buckley sitting at a microphone somewhere in this city in 1930, talking into the dark on behalf of people who needed someone to speak for them. She read about the eight days between his death and The first broadcast of a voice without a face. Some say The Shadow was based on him, but production schedules would suggest otherwise, since so little time between Buckley's death and the broadcast of The Shadow transpired. She thought about what it meant to choose silence as a weapon rather than accept it as a wound. "Motor City Mayhem! Bloody July. The corrupt mayor."

The Shadow. Whose work continued with, she looked up at the old man scanning his monitors, the Whisper. Not heroes, but equalizers.

She looked at the sketchbook in her hands. The new one. Given without explanation, the way everything in the last three days had been given. She opened it to the first page. Still blank. Still waiting.

She picked up her pencil. Jerry Buckley would be her first drawing.

She didn't draw Freeling. She didn't draw the library, the Underpass, the green door, or any of it. She drew a microphone. Old-fashioned, the kind she had seen in photographs of that era. Sitting alone in a sound office with no one behind it.

She looked at it for a moment.

Then she closed the sketchbook and stood up. It was time; her ride would be here in a minute.

A third clipping fell out, newer than the other but not new. A magazine piece, the paper slick and yellowed at the edges. It was about a radio program. She recognized the name from somewhere distant and childhood-adjacent, the kind of thing that existed in the background of old movies and older jokes.

The Shadow.

She read the relevant lines slowly.

The Shadow had debuted on radio on July 31, 1930.

She looked at the date on the Free Press mimeograph.

July 24, 1930.

Eight days.

She stood in the flat white light of the Archive Room with both pieces of paper in her hands and felt something move through her that she did not have a word for yet. She was fifteen years old, and she had survived something that was supposed to erase her. Something similar had erased Jerry Buckley.

Someone had left her an envelope with her name on it in precise dark blue ink, and inside it two pieces of paper and no explanation at all.

It hadn't been Whisper. He'd been with her.

She tucked everything away. She did not need an explanation.

She watched Whisper work, tweaking things here and there. Sending texts to this number or that. For a super old person, he was gifted with understanding and using technology.

She folded both clippings carefully and pressed them inside the new sketchbook. The history and the evidence and the portrait, all together now, held in the same binding he had given her.

She came back around the shelving unit. He was still at the table. Still not turned around.

She stood behind him for a moment.

"How old were you," she said, "in 1930?"

A long silence.

"That will keep too," he said. “I am old, but not that old. But the shadow of Buckley’s work is passed on. You know where to find me. Please see to it that no one else does. I don’t clear out as much corruption as I would like, but I value the little bit I can do.”

She almost smiled. “I wouldn’t out this place. I know you said you’re not a hero, but you are to me.”

“That too will pass.”

She tucked the sketchbook under her arm and looked toward the green door at the top of the ramp.

The equipment hummed. The fluorescent lights buzzed faintly.

"I think you have a good head on your shoulders and could be trained to help," he said. And something in the two words suggested he did not entirely mind.

“That’s why you brought me here.” She stood toward the door.

“Yes.”

“Because of your work, the Shadow’s work needs to continue.”

“Yes. Shade. That’s your new name, by the way. Because that is where you dwell, have dwelled over the last 48 hours.”

She smiled. “Shade. I like it.”

“You’ll find life a little easier, don’t get slack. Study that.” He pointed with his crooked finger. “You have a good start, don’t stop.”

“I won’t.”

She went up the ramp, opened the green door, and stepped out into the Detroit morning.

Above her, the city moved, as it always had, indifferent and alive and full of people who did not know what had happened in the last three days beneath one of its forgotten buildings.

A black Lincoln Navigator pulled up. “Miss Stevenson? I presume?” The driver said, getting out to open the door for her.

Chapter Thirteen

Marley's English Project, Six Months Later

A Report on Gerald "Jerry" Buckley *Submitted by Marley Stevenson, Mr. Granger, 3rd period, 10th grade English. Final English Project.*

Gerald Emmett Buckley was a radio announcer at station WMBC in Detroit, Michigan. On July 23, 1930, three men walked across the lobby of the LaSalle Hotel on Woodward Avenue, surrounded his chair, and shot him eleven times. Six of those bullets struck the back of his head within an area of four inches. He was thirty-nine years old.

Nobody was ever convicted.

I chose Jerry Buckley for this assignment because I have recently spent a lot of time studying Detroit's information flow as a business, and because I've been contemplating what it costs a person to tell the truth when it might be easier and safer to remain silent.

Buckley called his radio listeners the "Common Herd." He meant it as a compliment, since "herd" did not have the same political meaning today as it did during Prohibition. He believed that ordinary people, the ones who showed up for work, tried to pay their bills, watching their city fall apart around them, deserved someone in their corner. He campaigned on air for old-age pensions and jobs for the unemployed. He investigated corruption and named names. He received threatening letters and kept getting on the microphone anyway. When a friend urged him to make a list of everyone who might want him dead, Buckley thought about it and said, "I'll be alright."[1]

He was not alright.

Detroit in the summer of 1930 was not a safe place to tell the truth. "Bloody July" is what historians call those weeks. Eleven people were killed by gangsters in nineteen days.[2] Buckley's murder was the eleventh. He had just finished his final broadcast announcing that Mayor Charles Bowles had been recalled from office, and he went downstairs to the hotel lobby to read the newspaper, and that was where they found him.[3]

One hundred and fifty thousand people attended his funeral.[4]

The murder was never solved. The trial produced conflicting testimonies from witnesses who contradicted each other, a key witness who refused cross-examination and fought with reporters, and a man who had disappeared after the shooting and reappeared a week before the trial to say that the three defendants were not the men he saw.[5] The jury could not reach a verdict. The LaSalle Hotel where Buckley died was eventually demolished. The corner of Woodward and Adelaide is residential now, part of a complex called Woodward Place.[6]

I think about the fact that he knew. His secretary said he never got into a taxicab without checking the driver's face, never got out without scanning the street. He knew someone was watching him, and he kept broadcasting anyway, because people were listening, and because he thought the truth was worth more than his own safety.

I do not know if he was right about that. I am not sure there is a clean answer. I do think that sometimes you are thrown into situations that leave you no choice, and most of us believe that is directed at something wrong we have done, but life isn't that simple. Sometimes your situation leaves you no choice but to be the hero, whether you like it or not.

What I know is that a hundred and fifty thousand people stood at his funeral in the middle of a Depression and said that his life mattered. That is not nothing. That is, maybe, the whole point.

Works Cited

Murray, Riley. "After 25 Years, the Question is Still Unanswered: Who Killed Jerry Buckley?" *Detroit Free Press,* July 17, 1955.

"Killing of Buckley Arouses Detroit." *The New York Times,* July 24, 1930, p. 1.

Ibid.

Walsh, Kevin. "Death of a Whistleblower: Detroit's Bankruptcy, Edward Snowden and Jerry Buckley." *HuffPost,* September 27, 2013.

Brown, Susan. "After a Half-Century, This Detroit Murder Remains a Mystery." *Detroit Free Press,* July 27, 1980.

Vachon, Paul. "Murder of Beloved Radio Host Jerry Buckley Rocked Detroit in 1930. It's Still Unsolved." *Detroit Free Press,* October 3, 2021.

www.ingramcontent.com/pod-product-compliance
Lightning Source LLC
LaVergne TN
LVHW051013080826
845145LV00009B/2596

* 9 7 8 1 9 7 2 4 9 2 0 4 8 *